KU-303-683

Some words about kittens:

"AAARGGHHH! My fingers have fallen off!"
Harrison

☆

"Where's my sardine gone???!!"
Derek

☆

"Miaow, squeak, purr, yum!"
Mini Moo

☆

"Look at my face. Look at my ankles!!!!"
Daisy's mum

☆

"¡Hasta el año que viene, Daisy!"
Angelo

More Daisy adventures!

Kes Gray

DAISY

and the trouble with

KITTENS

RED FOX

RED FOX

UK | USA | Canada | Ireland | Australia
India | New Zealand | South Africa

Red Fox is part of the Penguin Random House group of companies
whose addresses can be found at global.penguinrandomhouse.com.

www.penguin.co.uk
www.puffin.co.uk
www.ladybird.co.uk

First published 2009
This edition published 2020

002

Character concept copyright © Kes Gray, 2009
Text copyright © Kes Gray, 2009
Illustration concept copyright © Nick Sharratt, 2009
Interior illustrations copyright © Garry Parsons, 2009
Cover illustrations copyright © Garry Parsons, 2020

The moral right of the author and illustrator has been asserted

Set in VAG Rounded Light 15pt/23pt
Printed in Great Britain by Clays Ltd, Elcograf S.p.A.

A CIP catalogue record for this book is available from the British Library

ISBN: 978-1-782-95969-4

All correspondence to
Red Fox, Penguin Random House Children's
One Embassy Gardens, 8 Viaduct Gardens
London SW11 7BW

MIX
Paper from
responsible sources
FSC
www.fsc.org   FSC® C018179

Penguin Random House is committed to a
sustainable future for our business, our readers
and our planet. This book is made from Forest
Stewardship Council® certified paper.

To Minnow.
We miss you.

Chapter 1

The **trouble with *gatitos*** is they are soooooooooo cute!!!!

"*Gatitos*" is Spanish for kittens! The waiter I met on our holiday told me.

If *gatitos* looked like slugs instead of kittens, then what happened on our Spanish holiday would never ever have happened. No way José.

If *gatitos* had slimy skin and gungy

1

bits, instead of cute little whiskers and cute little eyes and cute little noses and cute little paws and cute little everything elses, then I definitely wouldn't have got into trouble on holiday.

I wouldn't have stroked them or given them names or anything.

Or given them bits of my Spanish ham.

How was I to know there would be kittens in our hotel in Spain? Especially kittens that wanted another mum? There weren't any kittens in the holiday magazine that my mum showed me before we went. There were just pictures of our hotel and a swimming pool and a beach. There wasn't one kitten in any of the pictures anywhere.

If you ask me, if hotels have kittens as well as swimming pools, then they should say so in their magazines. But they don't. At least our hotel didn't.

WHICH ISN'T MY FAULT!

Chapter 2

Me and my mum hardly ever go on holiday. We would like to but the trouble is, going on holiday costs ever such a lot of money. Even when it's foreign money, it still costs a lot.

The **trouble with things that cost a lot of money** is you have to save up for them.

If you're trying to save up a lot, it can take ages! You need a huge piggy bank if you're saving up for something as big as a holiday.

Luckily something really really good happened. My nanny and grampy had some money they didn't want, so they gave it to my mum instead!

Mum was really pleased when Nanny and Grampy came round to our house to tell her. She was so pleased she burst out smiling, and then gave them about ten really big kisses!

Then she gave me a big kiss too, and said, "Daisy! Pack your bags – we're going on a summer holiday!"

The **trouble with big kisses** is they can be a bit too big sometimes. The big kiss Mum gave me nearly squashed my nose off!

Once I'd made sure my nose was still on, I ran straight upstairs to my bedroom to pack my bags like Mum asked.

The **trouble with packing your bags** is I've only got a school bag. Actually it's a rucksack, but it's still not that big.

By the time I'd got my toys and my football in it, I didn't have any room left for holiday clothes!

Then my mum came into my bedroom and said, "Daisy, I didn't mean pack your bags right now."

She meant, *Daisy, start thinking about what you would like to take on holiday*, because she hadn't actually booked the hotel yet, and we didn't actually know where we would be going yet, and we wouldn't actually be going anywhere for about a month!

Then my nanny and grampy came into my bedroom and said it would probably be better if I left my football at home and bought a blow-up beach ball instead. That would give me much more room in my rucksack.

Then they gave ME some holiday money too! Ten pounds, they gave me! All to myself! I'd never been so rich!

Grampy said I could find a beach ball to buy when I got to the holiday place. And a bucket and spade if I wanted. Mum said I might even be able to afford a fishing net too.

But then I had the idea of buying some scuba gear. Or a small yacht. Then, once I'd thought about it a bit more, I couldn't decide what I was going to buy.

That's the **trouble with being rich.**

There are far too many things you can afford. Especially when you're going on holiday!

Then Mum said that it would probably be best to wait until we actually got to where we were going and then decide. If we waited till we got to where we were going, I might find something else to spend my money on.

Something I hadn't thought of.

So I waited.

And waited.

And waited and waited.

About four and a half blimmin' weeks!

Chapter 3

The **trouble with waiting about four and a half blimmin' weeks to go on holiday** is it makes you go all trembly and excited. Especially when you've found out where you're going!

I thought we were going to go to Cornwall again, which is in England, so when my mum told me we were going to Spain, my eyeballs nearly popped out and rolled across the carpet!

Spain isn't even in England. It's in a completely different country of the world!

Plus, to get to Spain you can't go in your car, you have to fly there in an actual aeroplane! An actual aeroplane that takes off and flies through the actual sky and goes above the actual clouds and everything!

When I found out I was going to be going on an actual aeroplane to actual Spain for my actual summer holiday, even my trembles got the trembles!

"Now don't get over-over-excited like you normally do, Daisy," said Mum. "You know what happens when you get over-over-excited."

But I couldn't stop myself.

I rang my best friend Gabby straight away to tell her the news, but she wasn't in.

So I ran all the way, three doors up the road, to my second best friend Dylan's house to tell him instead.

Dylan has been to loads of places in the world. He is nine though. (And he's got a snake.)

Dylan told me Turkey was good, Egypt was too hot, Clacton was wicked, especially the slot machines, but Spain was definitely the best.

And guess what!

That's exactly what Gabby said when I saw her too. Not about Turkey and Egypt and Clacton, because she hadn't been there. But about Spain. Gabby had definitely been to Spain. She had photos and a Spanish teddy to prove it!

The **trouble with Spanish teddies** is they're a bit stiff. And not very cuddly. Plus they don't look like teddies, they look more like cows.

Gabby said they don't have teddies that look like teddies in Spain. They only have teddies that look like black bulls or donkeys.

Black bulls and stiff donkeys? I definitely wasn't going to spend my holiday money on a teddy like that. I was going to spend it on something much better.

Like a harpoon gun maybe. Or a jet ski!

Gabby told me that swimming pools in Spain had blow-up dolphins that you can sit on. And Spain had ice creams with gobstoppers full of bubble gum in them.

So then I got even more excited. But I still had ages to wait!

Which made me get even MORE EXCITED!!!!

Then Mum showed me a picture of the hotel where we would be staying!

And the beach we would be going to.

And the swimming pool we would be swimming in.

And the slide I would be sliding down.

And then she showed me where Spain was on the map.

And then a few days later she bought me a new swimming costume!

And the next week she bought me some new flip-flops.

And the week after that she bought me some special sun cream that would make my face turn blue!

And then the week after that it was almost time to go!

By the time we started doing the proper actual packing, my trembles were nearly shaking I was so excited!

Chapter 4

The **trouble with suitcases** is they won't shut. Not if you put too many things in them, they won't.

Mum said our suitcase would shut, but she was definitely wrong.

Even when she bounced up and down on it, our red suitcase wouldn't close.

"Sit on it with me, Daisy," she said.

So I did. But when we bounced up and down to make it close, the sun cream got squashed and squirted out all over the bed.

Luckily, it wasn't my special blue sun cream because I was going to need that for doing scary faces on holiday, but Mum still wasn't very happy.

Then she tried putting the suitcase on the floor and standing on it.

But standing on it didn't work either.

So she tried jumping on it.

21

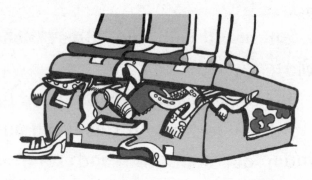

But this time the handle on her hairbrush snapped, and then, when she jumped up and down the next time, the heel broke off one of her favourite shoes.

I said she didn't need eight pairs of shoes to go on holiday, but Mum said she needed a pair for every day we were going to be there, plus a pair for emergencies.

So I asked if I could take my bike for emergencies too.

But she said no.

Then she opened the suitcase and started taking all my things out! Well, not ALL my things – she left all my holiday clothes inside, but she took out all my toys. Including my roller blades and my giant super-soaker water pistol!

Mum said roller blades wouldn't work on sand, and if I wanted to super-soak someone on holiday, then I could splash them with swimming-pool water instead.

So I said some of her shoes

wouldn't work on sand either, especially the ones with high heels, plus about eight of her dresses wouldn't work on sand either.

Mum said they weren't meant to work on sand, they were meant to work on dance floors.

In the end we gave up sitting and bouncing and jumping on our red suitcase, and borrowed an extra one from Nanny and Grampy instead. Not a red one; a brown one with a squeaky wheel.

That night, Mum said I could put some extra toys in my school rucksack too, as long as I promised to carry it all the way to Spain.

That's the **trouble with carrying rucksacks**. You can never get anyone to carry them for you.

So I only put a pad in, and some comics to read on the plane.

Plus my smallest teddy.

And a smallish giraffe.

Then, once I had added my pencil case and my favourite key ring with a monkey on it, I was all packed and ready to go! Then I started to feel

really really really excited.

"Mum, can I—?"

"No, you can't stay up late," said my mum, before I'd even got a chance to finish what I was saying. "The taxi will be picking us up at three a.m. to take us to the airport tomorrow, Daisy," she told me. "I want you to have an early night tonight."

That's the trouble with my mum.

She always knows what I'm going to say next.

Well, nearly almost always.

"And can I—?"

"And can you what?" asked my mum.

"And can I sleep in my clothes?" I asked. "Please, Mum, let me sleep in my clothes. Then I'll be all ready to go on holiday the moment you wake me up!"

The **trouble with me saying "Can I?"** is nearly always my mum says no.

But guess what! This time she didn't say no, she said yes!

"Good idea, Daisy," she said. "Anything that saves time in the morning is a good idea in my books!"

"Plus please can I—?"

"Plus please can you what now?" asked Mum, with a bit of a frown on her face this time.

"Plus please can I drive the aeroplane tomorrow?" I asked.

"No you can't, Daisy," she said. "Seven-year-olds do not drive aeroplanes to Spain."

Well, it was worth a try.

Chapter 5

The **trouble with taxis** is they are always late.

It was ten past three the next morning. I had got up, eaten my breakfast, brushed my hair, cleaned my teeth, put my trainers on, zipped up my rucksack, unzipped my rucksack (to check my monkey key ring was in there), zipped up my rucksack again, unzipped it again (to check I'd put a rubber in my pencil case), zipped it up again, unzipped it again (to talk to my teddy), zipped it up again, put my jacket on, put my rucksack on my back, taken my rucksack off my back (to see if my monkey key ring was still there), put my rucksack on again, walked round and round the lounge at least fifteen times, and the taxi STILL hadn't arrived!

Mum was starting to get a bit fidgety too, but just as she picked up the phone to find out where it was, the taxi pulled up outside our house.

"At last!" she said. "Come on, Daisy, it's time to go!"

The taxi driver got out of his car to help Mum with the suitcases.

It was really dark and exciting outside our house. Everyone in the whole street was asleep except for me and Mum! Even the birds were still asleep!

When we drove past Dylan's house, I looked up at his bedroom curtains and imagined him snoring in his bed. Then I imagined his pet snake Shooter curled up on his heat pads too.

Being the only one awake in the street was reeeeeeally exciting!

When we got to a bigger road, we saw that other people in England were awake too. Not many, but at least twelve. I asked my mum if she thought they were all going on a summer holiday too. She said that some might be, but most were probably going to work or coming home from work.

I didn't know people went to do jobs that early in the morning. Or came home from them that late.

Mum said that milkmen do very early jobs, so that when they put the milk on your doorstep, they can make sure it's nice and fresh.

That's the **trouble with milk** – if you don't keep it fresh it goes all lumpy and mouldy.

And it smells. I sniffed some

mouldy milk when I was round at Gabby's house once, and both our noses nearly fell off it was so stinky.

Now we only sniff nice things. Like Playdoh.

The **trouble with my mum at half-past three in the morning** is she doesn't want to play games or anything.

I thought playing games in the taxi would be really exciting, but Mum just said that she was too tired.

Then she said, "Daisy, we've got a long day ahead. Why don't you close your eyes and try and get some more sleep before we get to the airport?"

SLEEP? When you're going to AN AIRPORT? How could anyone possibly sleep when they are in an actual taxi, going to an actual airport with an actual aeroplane that's going to fly you all the way to ACTUAL SPAIN?!!!!

I couldn't even close my eyes!

So I played I-Spy on my own.

The **trouble with playing I-Spy on your own** is you always know the answers.

So I counted lampposts instead.

The **trouble** **with** **counting lampposts** is there are too many, so I counted horses instead.

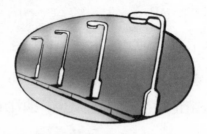

The **trouble with counting horses** is there weren't any, so I imagined I was Spanish instead.

The **trouble** **with** **imagining** **you're Spanish** is it's really hard if you haven't been to Spain before.

I could imagine where I lived. I lived in a smallish castle with palm trees and coconuts in the garden. It was very hot, the sun was always shining and the sky was really blue, but my face was even bluer because of my sun cream. I had two pets. My black bull was called Blackie and my donkey was called Giddyup.

Plus my name wasn't Daisy – it was Daisyella, because in Spain children are only allowed to have Spanish-sounding names.

My best friends were called Gabbyella instead of Gabby and Pepe instead of Dylan.

My favourite food was sausagellas with tomatoella sauce.

My favourite drink was fizzy orangella and my favourite crisps were smoky baconella.

But after that I couldn't think of anything else Spanish, so I watched my mum dribbling instead.

The **trouble with dribble** is it always comes out when you're asleep.

I don't know why, because if you go to sleep, then your dribble should go to sleep too really.

But it doesn't. At least my mum's dribble doesn't. My mum's dribble goes really dribbly when she's asleep. Especially when she starts snoring.

The **trouble with snoring** is when they get to be big snores, they sound like a pig eating porridge.

And they make your dribble wobble.

I thought the taxi driver might crash the car when Mum started dribbling AND snoring so I gave her a nudge with my elbow.

The **trouble with nudging someone with your elbow** is it makes them jump if they're asleep. And it makes their dribble go all over their face.

Mum wiped her dribble off really quickly, sat up straight and pretended she hadn't been asleep in the first place.

But I could see her eyes closing again in the reflection in the taxi window. So I didn't nudge her again after that. Not until we arrived at the airport.

Chapter 6

The **trouble with arriving at airports** is it's really hard not to jump up and down! Even if you've got your seat belt on!

Arriving at airports is so exciting! All the buildings are big and square and made out of concrete. And all the lights are really bright. Plus there are absolutely loads of people everywhere.

Plus if you look up in the sky, you can see actual planes coming in to land and other ones that are taking off! You should see how big aeroplanes look when they are close up! I thought one was going to land on our head!

When we got out of our taxi, there were people pushing trolleys into the airport and people pushing trolleys out of the airport all over the place! All the people going in had long trousers on but some of the people coming out were wearing shorts! And flip-flops! And they had suntans and everything!

Mum said the people coming out of the airport had been on their holidays and the people going in were about to start their holidays.

Just like us!

After Mum had paid the taxi man, we went and got a trolley all of our own!

The **trouble with trolleys all of your own** is they make you want to have a ride on them.

Mum said you aren't really meant to ride on trolleys at the airport in case you fall off, but once we'd put our suitcases on, she let me climb on top!

It was brilliant!!!!

Then guess what we had to do! We had to go through some really big

turning doors! Not normal doors like you get at home, but great big ones that turned round and round like a roundabout. It was so much fun, Mum and me went round in circles three times before we went in!

And then guess what!

We had to go along a really long piece of floor that actually moved! It was just like moving carpet, except it wasn't made of carpet. It was black like rubber. Anyway, you didn't have to walk on it or anything. All you had to do was stand on it and it carried you all the way inside!

I'd never seen inside an airport before. It was amazing!

I'd never seen so many people

before either. Or trolleys! Or suitcases! Or queues! There were queues everywhere. Really long ones too.

It took us ages to get our passports looked at, and ages to get our suitcases weighed, and ages to get our tickets from the lady, but I didn't care. We were in an ACTUAL AIRPORT, going to ACTUAL SPAIN on an ACTUAL SUMMER HOLIDAY for SEVEN WHOLE ACTUAL DAYS!!!!!

I'd have queued for a hundred years to do that! (I don't think Mum would have though.)

That's the **trouble with queues**. You have to be quite small to enjoy them.

It's the same with airport floors.

The **trouble with airport floors** is they make you want to do skids.

Once we'd done all our queuing I just had to do some big skids! Mum said I shouldn't do skids in airports because I might knock someone over or crash into a trolley, but I couldn't stop myself. One skid I did went about five metres! (That was a standing-up skid.)

Another one I did went about seven and a half metres. (That was a skidding-on-my-knees skid.)

But then the next skid I did went straight into a man carrying a cup of coffee.

I didn't go very far on that one, but his coffee did.

His coffee went about eleven metres. All over the floor. And down his shirt.

That's the **trouble with people who drink coffee.** They're always drinking it where children need to do skids.

So I had to stop doing skids after that.

And I had to say sorry.

Plus my mum had to buy the man

another coffee. But not another shirt.

She did offer to buy him another shirt, but the man said he would be fine when he had dried out. And anyway, it serves him right really, for not looking where he was going.

Chapter 7

The **trouble with x-ray machines** is people aren't allowed to lie down and go through them.

I wanted my mum to lie down and go through the x-ray machine. That way I would have been able to see her being a skeleton!

That's what x-ray machines do. They see right through the outside of things and show you all the bits on the inside.

Mum said we were only allowed to put our bags and jackets and shoes through the x-ray machines.

But the **trouble with bags and jackets and shoes** is they don't have skeletons in the middle. Which means they're not as good.

Once we'd put our bags on the x-ray machine we had to walk through a special rectangle that bleeped if you were carrying daggers or machine guns or swords or key rings with monkeys on.

When I went bleep, I thought I was going to be arrested and sent to prison or something, but when the x-ray man found my key ring in my pocket he let me go free.

Which is lucky really because prison is nowhere near as good as Spain.

After I'd stopped bleeping, my mum made me put my monkey key ring in my rucksack, and then we went to the airport shops. I couldn't wait to spend my holiday money!

The **trouble with airport shops** is most of them don't have scuba gear in them.

Or small yachts.

Mum said that if I saw anything else in the shops that I wanted to spend my holiday money on, I should let her know.

But I couldn't see any harpoon guns or jet skis or ice creams with bubble gum in them either.

I did see a strawberry Cornetto that looked quite nice, but Mum said I wasn't allowed ice cream at six o'clock in the morning.

I wasn't allowed an underwater wristwatch either. Or a basketball net.

In the end I decided to save my

holiday money until I got to Spain. Which was lucky really, because I didn't know at the time that I would need it for the kittens.

The **trouble with seats in airport lounges** is when you try and lie across three seats at once, the gaps in between make you feel all uncomfortable.

Mum said I should sit up nicely and listen for our plane to be announced.

But other people were lying all over the seats. And they were grown-ups! One man with knots in his hair and a giant rucksack was lying across about six seats! So I didn't see why I couldn't.

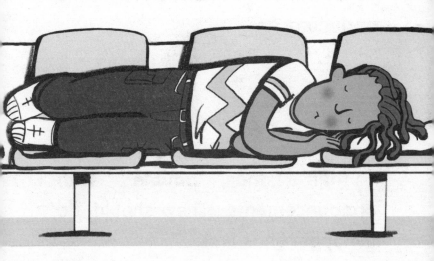

Except I thought I'd fall through the gaps, so I did sit up in the end.

The **trouble with airport announcers** is they always say the wrong plane. Loads of planes were taking off all the time to loads of holidays all over the world. But none of the announcements were for me and Mum!

That's the **trouble with announcements.** They should do the Spain ones first.

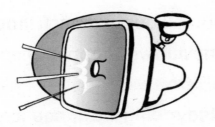

Mum told me that our flight number was MLG452 and that as soon as our plane had been cleaned and tidied and filled up with petrol, then there would be an announcement for us to get on our plane too.

I said I didn't mind going to Spain in a dirty plane or one that didn't have much petrol in it, but Mum said that wasn't a very good idea.

So we waited.

And waited and waited.

Until . . . just when I thought it would never ever happen . . .

IT DID!

The lady doing the announcements actually announced our actual plane to actual Spain!

"Time to go, Daisy!" said Mum. "We need to go to gate fifty-three. Gate fifty-three is where our plane will be taking off from soon!"

The **trouble with gate fifty-threes** is they feel like they are about fifty-three miles from the airport!

Mum said it was nothing like fifty-three miles away, but it felt like ever such a long walk to me.

That's the **trouble with small legs**. They start to ache much earlier than longer ones. Especially if you're carrying a rucksack.

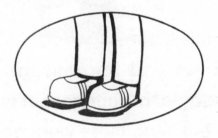

Except that's when I realized I wasn't!

I wasn't carrying my rucksack at all!

I'D LEFT MY RUCKSACK UNDER THE SEAT IN THE AIRPORT LOUNGE!!!

The **trouble with leaving rucksacks under seats in airport lounges** is you're not allowed to do it.

We ran and ran and ran all the way back to the lounge, but when we got to our seat, there were about five policemen moving people away from my school bag!!!!!

At first I thought someone had tried to steal my monkey key ring, but

then Mum went really red and said that the policemen were checking inside my school bag for a bomb!

The **trouble with bombs** is they can blow up, so I would never EVER put one in my school bag. Plus I don't know where to buy bombs.

Mum knew that, because she's my mum, but the policemen hadn't met me before so she had to tell them. Which made her go even redder than red.

At first the policemen did loads of frowns at her, then, before they gave me my rucksack back, they checked my mum for bombs too!

In front of loads and loads of people.

Mum said she'd never been so embarrassed in her life. Which is probably true.

Then there was another announcement. Except this time it didn't say the name of our aeroplane – it said OUR names instead! In big loud words right across the airport!

"QUICK, DAISY!" said Mum. "IT'S OUR LAST CALL! Run as fast as you can or we're going to MISS OUR PLANE!"

The **trouble with missing your plane** is it means you will miss your holiday too!

So we had to run all the way!

The **trouble with running all the way to gate fifty-three** is it makes your legs ache EVEN MORE! Plus it makes your face all hot and red, and your back all sticky.

By the time we got there, my mum could hardly speak she was so out of breath!

Plus her face was a new kind of red I'd never ever seen before.

"DON'T EVER LEAVE A BAG UNATTENDED IN AN AIRPORT AGAIN, DAISY!" was all she could manage to say.

"I'M SO EXCITED, I'M SO EXCITED, I'M SO EXCITED!!!" was all I could say back.

Chapter 8

The **trouble with aeroplanes** is all the seats should be by the windows. If all the seats in aeroplanes were by the windows, then everyone could look out.

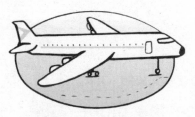

Mum said she didn't mind not looking out of the window because she'd looked out of an aeroplane window before, but I think putting seats in the middle of an aeroplane is silly.

Before we put our seat belts on we had to put our bags in a high-up cupboard above our seats.

Mum said that it was called an overhead locker and that once the plane had taken off, she would get my things out of my rucksack to play with.

Then we had to put our seat belts on.

The **trouble with seat belts** is you're not allowed to keep unclipping them and then doing them up again, and then unclipping them and doing them up again.

I got really good at undoing and doing up my seat belt, but then I got frowned at by an aeroplane lady. Then my mum said the plane wouldn't take off if I didn't leave my seat belt alone.

So I had to just do it up and not unclip it after that.

When we took off, my tummy went all funny. That's the **trouble with planes taking off** – they go so fast, your tummy can't keep up.

At first I nearly didn't look out of the window, but when I did it was brilliant! Everything on the ground had gone really small!

All the cars on the roads looked

like teensy toy ones and all the trees and fields looked like tiny broccolis inside little green squares.

Mum said the higher we got, the smaller everything would look.

And she was right, because then we went even higher! We went right up up up into the air above the actual clouds! Real ACTUAL clouds! Great big, fat, fluffy ones that looked like great big, fat oodles and oodles of white, fluffy cotton wool.

I wanted to get out of the plane and bounce about on them, but Mum said no one was allowed outside during the journey.

And anyway, we still had to keep our seat belts on.

That's the **trouble with seat belts**. If you take them off before you're allowed to, the aeroplane lady will come and tell you off.

When we were allowed to undo our seat belts, the captain driving the plane did an announcement. He said that we would soon be cruising at 37,000 feet and that a little bit later we were going to be given breakfast to eat, plus teas and coffees!

Then I decided I needed my pad and pencil case.

The **trouble with needing a pad and pencil case when they're in an overhead locker** is your mum has to undo her seat belt, get up, squeeze past the person she's sitting next to, reach up to the overhead cupboard and take the pad and pencil case out of your bag to give it to you.

The **trouble with needing a comic just after you've needed a pad and pencil case** is then your mum has to do it all over again.

Then I needed my giraffe. And then I needed my monkey key ring.

Which made her a little bit cross and the person she was sitting next to a little bit huffy and puffy.

So in the end Mum took my whole rucksack down from the overhead locker, gave it to me and told me to keep it under the seat in front of me.

So I did.

But then I needed to go to the loo.

The **trouble with loos on aeroplanes** is they are a bit small.

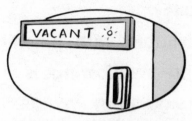

My loo at home has a bath in it and everything. The one on our aeroplane didn't even have a shower. Or EVEN a rubber duck!

Plus when I was sitting on the loo seat, my ears began to feel all shushy.

When I came out of the loo, my mum said that because we were so high up in the sky, the air pressure in our ears could begin to feel different. Then she told me to pinch my nose and swallow.

The **trouble with pinching your nose and swallowing** is it makes your ears go funny.

At first I didn't know what my ears were doing. They just felt wiggly inside and then everything went all loud.

Mum said it was called popping. But I didn't really like it.

I preferred not popping, or still shushy.

When we got back to our seats, I got my pad and pencils out of my bag to do some drawing.

"Draw an aeroplane," said Mum. "Draw a Spanish aeroplane."

Which was quite a good idea.

Except by then I'd worked out how to play with the tray in my seat.

The **trouble with aeroplane trays when they're right in front of you** is they really make you want to lower them and then push them up again.

And then lower them and push them up again.

And lower them and push them up again.

And lower them and push them up again.

Because it's really good fun.

Trouble is, the man sitting in the seat in front of me didn't know how to work his tray. So he got all jealous and huffy and puffy, and kept turning round to frown at me.

So Mum said I had better put my tray up and leave it up.

But I couldn't, because our breakfast had arrived!

Chapter 9

The **trouble with breakfasts on aeroplanes** is they don't do Coco Pops. They do sort-of-sausage and sort-of-bacon with sort-of-baked beans with sort-of-potatoes in a white plastic tray instead.

At first I didn't know what sort of breakfast it would be because I couldn't get the foil lid off, but when Mum pulled it off for me, I could see it wasn't Coco Pops.

So I just had my bread roll and orange juice instead.

Mum said that they probably wouldn't have Coco Pops in Spain either, and that not having Coco Pops on the plane would be good practice for not having Coco Pops in the hotel.

And she was right. Our hotel in Spain didn't do Coco Pops either.

But they did do Rice Krispies.

And they did kittens!

Not for breakfast. Just for stroking.

You should never put milk on kittens. It's all right to put milk in their saucer for them to drink, but you mustn't pour it actually on them.

Or sprinkle sugar on them.

Pouring milk or sprinkling sugar on kittens isn't allowed in Spain. Or any country in the world.

Otherwise you'll go to prison.

But stroking them is definitely all right. And cuddling them.

But playing with them is EVEN better!!!! If you ask me, playing with kittens is one of the best things you can do in the world.

Honestly, if I'd known there were going to be kittens at our hotel in Spain, I wouldn't have put any toys in my rucksack to play with AT ALL! Not even my monkey key ring!

I mean, who needs toys and teddies and key rings and colouring pens and pads in your rucksack when you've got kittens to play with?

NO ONE. That's who!

Still, at least the things in my rucksack gave me something to do on the plane.

I was going to play I-Spyella with Mum. I-Spyella is a new Spanish I-Spy game I have invented, but the trouble was, by the time I had drawn a Spanish aeroplane and some Spanish clouds and some really really high-up Spanish seagulls, my mum had fallen asleep and started snoring again.

Then she started dribbling again. Which I'm not sure is allowed on planes.

Luckily the aeroplane lady who gave us our breakfast didn't see the dribble, or she might have told the captain. And then the captain might have told everyone in the plane in an announcement!

"This is your captain speaking. We have a dribble alert in seat fourteen B. Please be careful that you don't get dribbled on when you walk past seat fourteen B, because the lady who is snoring next to the little girl in seat fourteen A is dribbling all over the place." Or something like that.

That's the **trouble with dribble alerts.** They can be really embarrassing. Especially if you're not allowed to jump off the plane.

Which you're definitely not.

Unless you've got a parachute.

So I just stayed quiet in my seat, played with my toys and coloured with my colouring pens.

While my mum dribbled.

Alllllllll

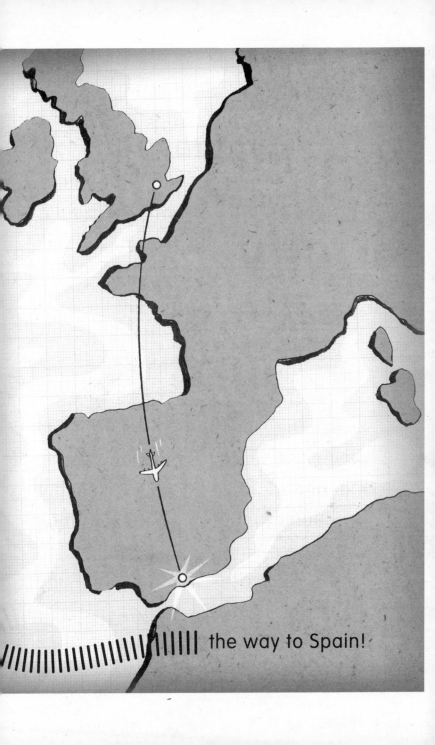

the way to Spain!

Chapter 10

The **trouble with airports in Spain** is they're a bit like the ones in England. Only hotter.

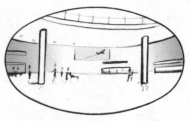

By the time we'd got off the plane and onto a bus, and driven to the airport building and given our passports to a grumpy Spanish man who never smiled, and then waited for our suitcases to come out, and

then found a trolley, and then lifted my rucksack onto the trolley, and then gone back to try and find Nanny and Grampy's squeaky-wheel, my face was really boiling!

That's the **trouble with sunshine in Spain.** It can burn straight through whole buildings!

And coaches!

The coach that drove us to our hotel after we'd left the airport was even hotter!

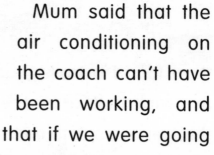 Mum said that the air conditioning on the coach can't have been working, and that if we were going to have a holiday in Spain, then we would just have to get used to hot temperatures.

If you ask me, my mum was really pleased it was so hot in Spain. Being hot in Spain makes the dribble on your shoulder dry up much much quicker.

It was faaaaaaaaar too hot in the coach for me though. Sitting on that coach was like being a jacket potato in a microwave. No, it was like being a chicken nugget in a red-hot oven.

Actually it was like being a crispy sausage that's fallen through the gap onto the barbecue coals, and then had loads more red-hot coals and some burning mustard put on top.

Anyway, that's probably why I fainted.

Mum said I didn't faint. I fell asleep.

But I definitely didn't.

Even if she said I did.

And I definitely didn't do any snoring.

Even if she said I did.

And I definitely didn't do any DRIBBLING!

Even Mum said I didn't do any dribbling. Anyway . . . BOY was I pleased when we arrived at our hotel!

And DOUBLE BOY was I excited when we got our suitcases off the coach and carried them inside!

You should have seen how Spanish everything was inside the hotel. Everywhere I looked there were Spanish things all over the place! There were Spanish people with Spanish name badges, there were great big Spanish pots with blue and white patterns on them, and massive posters of Spanish ladies doing Spanish dancing on the wall, plus there was a great big Spanish floor that you could do Spanish skids on, plus there were actual plants with lemons growing on them in actual Spanish . . . and you'll just never guess what else there was – growing out of the actual ground INSIDE the actual hotel – you'll just never guess . . .

Right up close to where we were actually standing!

And over by the window.

And over by all the other windows too!

There were real actual Spanish palm trees all over the place!

I reckon someone must have picked all the coconuts, because I couldn't see any, but all the other palm-tree bits were there! Great big trunks and great big palm-tree leaves, GROWING INSIDE our actual hotel!!

It was so exciting, I wanted to jump up and down and do skids and roly-polys all over the place! I wanted to do whoop-de-doops and fiddle-de-dellas and be jumpier and skiddier than I'd ever been before in my whole life!!!

And then I realized why!

I'd never been excited in Spanish before!

Mum said I should remember that I was English and try and keep my whoop-de-doops and fiddle-de-dellas to a minimum.

So I tried.

But then I saw our room!

And then I saw our balcony!

And then I saw the pool!

I could see the actual swimming pool from the actual balcony of our actual room!!!!

It had really blue water with people in it, plus a great big YELLOW SLIDE!

I've never put a swimming costume on so fast in my life!

Chapter 11

The **trouble with swimming costumes** is after you put them on you have to put sun cream on AS WELL.

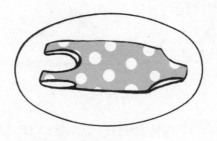

ALL THE TIME!

I couldn't wait to get into the pool and slide down the great big yellow slide into the water, but Mum said midday suns in Spain can roast you

like a turkey twizzler, so I wasn't allowed anywhere until I'd put my sun cream on.

The first time my mum put the sun cream on my face, I asked her to do me a really scary zombie face so I could frighten everyone in the pool.

Trouble is, when I got to the pool, lots of other children had scary blue zombie faces too!

One boy called Harrison even had a green face! Harrison was the first friend I met in the pool on holiday.

Actually, I didn't exactly meet him, I kind of landed on top of him. Which wasn't my fault, because he shouldn't have been doing shark impressions at the bottom of the yellow slide.

And anyway, it didn't hurt him when I landed on him. He just went under the water, disappeared for a while and then came up over by the getting-out steps.

Except he didn't get out, he stayed in.

At first I thought he might be a bit cross, but he wasn't cross at all. He smiled at me, emptied some water out of his swimming goggles, and then swam back towards me to say hello.

Harrison was eight, and ever such a good swimmer. And he could do proper dives into the deep end with his legs together. Plus he had a baby sister called Jo-Jo.

The **trouble with Jo-Jo** is she was only three, which meant she sank nearly all the time. Unless she had her rubber ring and armbands on.

Harrison said he was in charge of Jo-Jo when she was in the pool, especially when his mum and dad were lying down on the sun loungers with their eyes shut. Which was most of the time.

Harrison said that being in charge of Jo-Jo was the same as being a lifeguard, which is really good, because I'd never met an actual lifeguard before. Especially a green one!

When Harrison took me over to the shallow end to meet Jo-Jo, I met loads of other children on the way.

There was Carly, who was from Birmingham, Danny from Newcastle, Matty from Devon, and Cerise and Montague from Surrey. Cerise and Montague were really tanned because they'd already been at the hotel for a week.

Everyone else was mostly blue, except for Matty, who was blue with pink-and-red peely bits on his shoulders.

Everyone wanted to play with me, and everyone wanted to know my name. It was brilliant. I'd only been in the pool five minutes and I had seven new friends already!

Harrison and Jo-Jo were going to be my best friends on holiday though.

I'd never have found the kittens without Harrison and Jo-Jo. At least, not without Harrison and Jo-Jo's Frisbee.

Chapter 12

The **trouble with Frisbees** is you can never be *exactly* sure where they are going to go.

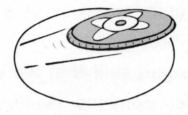

Every afternoon straight after lunch, me, Harrison, Matty, Carly, Cerise and Montague would meet by the slide with our T-shirts on, and then play Zombie Mermaids in the pool. Trouble is, boys don't usually want to be mermaids, even when they are zombie ones, so we couldn't really play Zombie Mermaids for very long.

Everyone wanted to play Frisbee-throwing though!

Especially when it was zombie Frisbee-throwing!

Montague said that we could all be Water Zombies (without being mermaids), and that our special zombie Frisbee was made out of red-hot lava. Which meant if you held it for too long all your fingers would melt off and sink to the bottom of the pool!

The **trouble with your fingers sinking to the bottom of the pool** is you can't hold Spanish lemonade or ice cream or anything, so if the Frisbee came to you, you had to throw it to someone else really fast!

The **trouble with throwing Frisbees really fast** is they can almost go into space. Especially if you're not standing in the pool when you throw it.

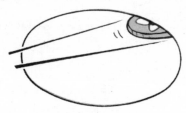

I did start off in the pool, and even when I was right up to my shoulders in water, I did some really good throws.

Trouble is, then I found a beetle floating in the water beside me.

Matty said it was a zombie headlouse from Deadland, but it wasn't. It was definitely a shiny black-and-green beetle from Spain. It splashed straight towards me and even touched my arm.

AND . . . its legs were still moving!

So I had to stop playing Zombie Frisbee for a moment, scoop it into a plastic cup and throw it out of the pool back onto the concrete.

The **trouble with throwing beetles out of swimming pools** is they land upside down!

The **trouble with beetles landing upside down** is then they can't turn themselves the right way up. They just stay upside down and wriggle and wriggle and wriggle. At least Spanish beetles do.

So I had to get out of the pool to help turn it over.

The **trouble with turning beetles over** is you can't really do it with your fingers. In case they nip you.

So you have to find a lolly stick to turn them over with instead. Then, once you've found a lolly stick, you have to concentrate really hard on getting the beetle's legs to grab on.

Which is quite hard.

And then you have to turn him over without him letting go.

Or he might fall off and land upside down again.

Which is even harder.

So when a zombie Frisbee comes to you, you don't really notice it at first.

And then, when everyone screams "Zombie Fingers!" at you, it really makes you jump.

And when you look round at everyone in the pool and they're telling you you've only got two seconds before your fingers melt off, it makes you really panic, pick up the zombie Frisbee and throw it away REALLY fast . . .

So fast that it goes right across the pool, straight over the sun loungers, in between some palm trees and over a fence.

Which wasn't my fault.

Except everyone said it was.

At first they laughed and splashed about and said it was really funny. Carly said I must have done a Turbo

Zombie Frisbee throw, Matty said I must have switched to Zombie Space Catapult Force, and Cerise said I'd thrown it so hard she was surprised my arm hadn't fallen off and landed in the pool! Which was the funniest.

But then Montague said I had to go and get the Frisbee back from over the fence. Which is wrong, because it wasn't even his Frisbee in the first place. It was Harrison and Jo-Jo's.

Then EVERYONE said I had to go and get the Frisbee back from over the fence, including Harrison and Jo-Jo. Because I was the one who had thrown it over.

Plus I was already out of the pool. (Thanks to that beetle!)

So I had no choice. I HAD to go and look for the Frisbee. Which meant I had to go behind the fence too.

The **trouble with fences** is they can be a bit strange when they're Spanish. Especially when you don't know what is on the other side.

So I asked Montague and Cerise to come with me.

But they wouldn't. Montague said

that his flip-flops were under the bed in his hotel room and that Spanish concrete was too hot for his feet.

Cerise said she wanted to have a go on the slide, Matty said he wanted to practise his duck diving, Carly said she was feeling a bit sunburned (which was definitely a lie, because she was bluer than any of us), and Danny said he needed to check the battery on his iPod.

Not including Jo-Jo, that only left Harrison.

I knew Harrison wouldn't let me down!

Chapter 13

The moment I saw the kittens I knew this was going to be my best holiday ever! Harrison said he saw them first because he was the first one to go through the gate in the fence. But he definitely didn't see them first.

He saw the Frisbee first, but it was me who saw the kittens. They were curled up under a bush beside some big metal dustbins.

The dustbins were really smelly and had Spanish flies buzzing all round them. But I didn't care. I only

cared about the kittens.

There were five! A grey one, a grey-and-white one, a black one, a black-and-white one and a ginger one! And there was a mummy one! The mummy one was kind of tabby coloured with a white tip on her tail. She was really skinny and, at first when she saw me, she looked a bit scared.

But when she realized I could do Spanish cat-talk, she was all right.

The **trouble with Spanish cat-talk** is only me and Spanish cats and kittens can understand it.

Harrison didn't understand it, and neither did Jo-Jo when we showed her the kittens the next day.

Spanish cat-talk is a mixture of sign language and squeaks. You either know how to do it or you don't. Which was a shame for Harrison and Jo-Jo because they didn't know how to do it, but then Harrison and Jo-Jo aren't as good with animals as I am.

Which is why it was better if I was more in charge of the kittens than them.

Even if Harrison was older than me.

Harrison said he definitely understood why the kittens had made their nest under a bush beside the dustbins. He said dustbins were full of things to eat, and so being next to one would mean they could always get food anytime they wanted it.

Which isn't true.

Because the **trouble with Spanish dustbins** is kittens can't get the lids off. Neither can mummy cats. Because the lids are too heavy and high up.

Which is probably why the kittens looked so skinny too. Especially the littlest black one.

I was the first one to touch her. She was soooOOOOOOOOOOO CUTE!

I was a bit nervous at first in case the mummy cat tried to scratch me. But after I'd squeaked to explain that I was only going to be kind to her kittens, and that later on I would come back and give them some food, she let me crouch down beside the bush, put my hand in and stroke them.

Then she even let me pick up one of her kittens!

The **trouble with picking up a Spanish kitten** is other people always want to have a hold too.

I'd only had the black one in the palm of my hand for about ten seconds before Harrison said it was his turn to hold him now.

So I had to let him. Otherwise it wouldn't have been fair.

Harrison said he thought he might have suddenly found the powers

to speak Spanish cat-talk, but he definitely hadn't.

Harrison's squeaks didn't sound like Spanish cat-language at all.

They sounded more like Russian hamster-language, if you ask me.

But I didn't tell him that. Because that wouldn't have been very fair either. Or kind.

So at first I only got a little hold of the black kitten.

And no holds of the other kittens at all!

Because before I could reach under the bush to get another one, Angelo came out of the back door of the pool bar and found us over by the dustbins.

Angelo is my favourite Spanish waiter in the world. He was really nice and friendly to us all the time we were on holiday. But the first time he met us, he said children weren't allowed around the dustbins, and he would get told off if he didn't ask us to leave.

Which I don't think was true either.

If you ask me, the reason he wanted us to go back to the pool had nothing to do with the dustbins. If you ask me, Angelo just wanted us

to go so he could smoke a cigarette without anyone seeing.

I'm definite about it actually, because I saw him hide a cigarette behind his back when he saw us. Plus when he asked us our names, there was smoke coming up from over his shoulder.

The **trouble with smoking cigarettes** is they can kill you. Whatever language you smoke them in, they can kill you deader than dead.

Cigarettes have got bad stuff inside them that can clog up your whole body and stop you breathing. And they can turn your teeth yellow.

And your hair.

My mum says that my granddad, who died before I was born, used to smoke, and the front of his hair went really yellow. Then he got a smoking disease and he died.

Like my dad.

Except my dad didn't die of smoke.

Or cigarettes.

He died of a car crash. When I was little.

But I don't remember. I've never remembered.

I hardly remember anything about when I was little.

I will remember never ever to smoke though.

Not in English or Spanish or any language. Which is why I had to tell Angelo off.

When Angelo found out Harrison and I had seen his cigarette, he dropped it on the ground and squashed the smoke out of it with the heel of his shoe.

Then he promised us he would never ever smoke a cigarette again. So we decided to like him. And he decided to like us!

It was Angelo who told us that the Spanish word for "never ever" was "no way José".

And that the Spanish word for kittens was *"gatitos"*!

It was Angelo who told us that the kittens were about ten weeks old, and that they had actually been born under the actual bush beside the actual dustbins!

It was Angelo who told us that he didn't know where the daddy cat was, and that Spanish daddy cats weren't very good at looking after kittens.

And it was Angelo who told us to keep the kittens a secret when we went back to the pool to play with our friends.

He said that if lots of children found out there were kittens behind the fence, then they would all want to see them and stroke them and pick them up and everything.

Then he would end up with lots of children around the dustbins.

Which meant he REALLY would get into trouble.

Plus the mummy cat might not like it.

Which meant he would have to lock the gate in the fence for good. Which meant we wouldn't be able to open it. Which meant we would never see the kittens again! Never ever!

So Harrison and me decided there and then: when we got back to the pool with the Frisbee, the five little Spanish *gatitos* behind the fence would be our five little secrets.

We wouldn't tell absolutely ANYONE about the cute little *gatitos* AT ALL! (Except for Jo-Jo and my mum.)

Chapter 14

The **trouble with my mum** is she gets jealous.

Not about kittens. About me having so many new friends.

Before I'd even got back into the pool with the Frisbee, she called me over to see her.

At first I thought she was going to tell me off for going behind a Spanish fence with Harrison, but what she had to say was much worse than that.

I couldn't believe it. Just because I'd made fourteen new friends on holiday (seven normal ones, six furry ones and Angelo), my mum decided she wanted to make a new friend too.

His name was Derek.

And he was a man.

The **trouble with men** is they might try to be my mum's boyfriend.

Which is yuk because my mum goes all different when she might be getting a boyfriend.

And she puts more make-up on.

The **trouble with my mum putting more make-up on** is it stops boyfriends from seeing how old she is in real life.

If you ask me, my mum is far too old to go out with a boyfriend. In fact, if you ask me, my mum is far too old to go out at all.

Except with me.

Like to the zoo or the shops.

Mum said that I was being silly, and that Derek and she were just good friends.

She said she had met him at the pool bar the day before. She said that Derek was very charming and very nice and would very much like to meet me!

I still didn't really want to meet him though.

I'd much rather have gone to dinner with the kittens.

Then Mum told me I HAD to meet Derek! In fact she'd already

made a date with him!

On Thursday night . . . which was only THREE days away!

Without even asking me first!

I was so cross, I nearly didn't tell her about the kittens.

And when I did tell her about the kittens, guess what she said next! She said that they sounded very nice, and that I should put on my best skirt and top when we went to dinner with Derek.

Which made me even crosser! One minute I was talking about the kittens and now we were talking about Derek again!

So I went and sat under a different umbrella.

How could she!

Just when I'd gone and found the best things I'd ever found in my life, she had to go and start putting on more make-up.

I was so cross, I could hardly think of any names to call the kittens at all!

Every time I tried to think of a really good kitten name, the name Derek kept coming into my head instead!

Derek, Derek, Derek, Derek and Derek.

Then I got so boiling cross, I had to go and jump in the pool to cool down.

Luckily the pool water really helped a lot. So did Harrison, once he'd told the others he wasn't playing Frisbee any more.

Miffy, Marble, Midnight, Mini Moo and Smoky. That's what the kittens' names would be!

Chapter 15

When Mum and me went for our dinner in the hotel that evening, the only thing I could think about was the kittens. They were soooo small and soooo skinny and soooo hungry and soooo under–a-bush-beside-a-dustbin . . . I just HAD to get them something really nice to eat.

That's why I took loads of octopus and anchovies from the buffet.

Anchovies are like tiny little fishes in slimy sauce, just right for growing kittens, and octopus is like . . .

Well, little bobbly bits of, er . . . octopus just right for growing kittens too.

At least Harrison said they would be, when we were standing with our plates in the buffet queue.

Harrison said he reckoned cats would absolutely love octopus and anchovies because they were made of fish. But then he said that he wouldn't actually be able to put any on his plate because his mum and dad would get suspicious.

That's the **trouble with octopus and anchovies**. Children can't eat them without looking suspicious.

Which meant my mum would be suspicious of my octopus and anchovies too.

So I hid them under a big pile of lettuce!

When I sat down at my table with a great big pile of lettuce, my mum's eyes nearly popped out of her head.

"What on earth have you got there, Daisy?" she asked.

"I fancied a lettuce salad," I said.

"A LETTUCE SALAD?" she said. "A LETTUCE BLOOMING SALAD?!" she said.

"HELLO, DEREK," she said.

That's when I met Derek for the first time.

Actually I was quite pleased to meet him because he took my mum's mind right off my lettuce.

"How are you, Derek?" said my mum, jiggling her earrings with the back of her hand and then fluttering her make-up at him like a soppy person.

"Daisy meet Derek, Derek meet Daisy," she said.

The **trouble with extra-long nostril hairs** is they make you look like a troll.

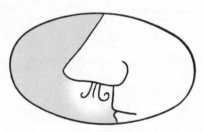

The **trouble with even medium-sized ear hairs** is they make you look like you've escaped from a zoo.

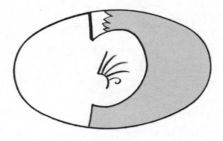

Apart from that, Derek didn't look too bad. His hair was a bit grey, his nose was a bit big, but his teeth were quite straight and he had a quite nice watch on.

Except then he did a wink.

The **trouble with winks** is strangers think they will make children like them.

Except they don't.

As far as I'm concerned, any stranger who winks at me is a total idiot.

"I believe I am going to have the pleasure of taking you and your lovely mum to dinner, Daisy," said Derek, stretching his arm across my anchovies for a handshake.

The **trouble with handshakes** is they don't work with one hand.

So I had to give him *my* hand to shake.

After we'd done the shake, Derek did ANOTHER wink!

Then he put his other hand on my mum's shoulder and whispered, "Are we still all right for Thursday?"

Then my mum went all soppy again and said that we couldn't wait

to go out for dinner with him.

Which was a lie.

"Where would you like to go?" asked Derek. "I know a lovely little Spanish tappers bar by the sea front."

"That would be lovely, Derek!" said my mum.

Which was another lie. In fact, the last thing on earth I wanted to do on my holiday was go Spanish tapping with Derek. Whatever Spanish tapping is.

"Thursday it is then!" said Derek, winking at me for a THIRD TIME, and then leaving us alone.

Nostril hairs, ear hairs and three winks!!! There was no way I was going to like Derek!

"Do we haaaaaaaave to go???" I said, hoping that my mum would change her mind and never see Derek again.

"Yes, we do haaaaaaaave to

go," said Mum. "Derek is a perfectly lovely man, and we will have a perfectly lovely evening with him on Thursday."

Except we didn't.

THANKS TO THE KITTENS!

Chapter 16

Apart from Derek and his winks, our holiday just got better and better after I'd found the kittens!

Well, mine did. Mum says hers just got worse and worse.

I used my special Spanish cat-talk to find out all about my little *gatitos*!

All the kittens liked licking the anchovies, but no one really liked the octopus.

The mummy cat told me that octopus was a bit chewy for growing kittens and that I should try stealing some different meaty things from the buffet.

Miffy told me she preferred chicken to beef, Marble said he quite liked prawns without their shells on.

Midnight asked me to take the bones out of the sea bream, and Smoky told me that if I could get him some really big bits of tuna that would be even better.

Plus Mini Moo asked me to take all the milk out of the milk jugs at breakfast.

So I did!

Well, me and Harrison did.

The trouble with hunting for meat is you have to make sure nobody sees you.

Every chance we got, we nabbed some meat for the kittens.

We got spicy sausage from the tops of Carly's mum and dad's pizza, Spanish ham from my mum's *Olé!* salad, some tuna mayonnaise out of Matty's mum's sandwich, and a whole sardine off Derek's plate when he was talking to my mum.

And no one ever saw us!

Well, not at first they didn't.

Angelo kept the gate unlocked for us every day, so whenever we wanted to visit or feed the kittens, we could.

And so could Jo-Jo.

So for Harrison, me and now Jo-Jo, EVERY DAY of our holiday was *GATITO* DAY!

We still played with Carly, Cerise, Montague, Matty and Danny in the pool. But we never ever gave away the secret of the kittens. No way José!

No one even got suspicious. Because whenever we wanted to see

the kittens we just threw
the Frisbee over the
fence! So nobody
ever knew!

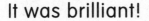

It was brilliant!

I even thought of something to spend my holiday money on that was brilliant too . . .

Kitten food! Real actual proper tins of it that you could buy in the supermarket down by the beach. Mum said kitten food was a silly thing to spend all my holiday money on. She said I should spend my holiday money on postcards or a beach ball or a sunhat.

But after Harrison and me got caught walking out of the evening buffet with a whole salmon, we were banned from stealing any more food from anywhere in the hotel by the hotel manager.

And the pool bar manager.

And our mums.

We couldn't even leave our tables without opening our napkins!

So I JUST HAD to spend ALL my holiday money on proper kitten food. Otherwise the kittens would have died of nothing to eat!

So the next morning after breakfast, Mum took me into the town to look at some real Spanish shops.

Chapter 17

The **trouble with real Spanish shops** is most of them don't sell kitten food at all!

The shops Mum kept taking me to only sold clothes!

Mum said she wanted to find a nice summer dress that she could wear to the tappers bar with Derek on Thursday evening.

Which made me even crosser.

I mean, how could anyone think about buying summer dresses to tap in when five little kittens were starving of something to eat back at the hotel?

Then she started looking for some new shoes!

She'd already put eight pairs in the suitcase; now she was looking for another pair!

It was a good job there was really cold air conditioning in the supermarket, otherwise I would have exploded like a hot-air balloon when I got there.

Mum said that if I didn't chill a bit, she would stick my head in the freezer compartment with the frozen peas.

But Spain doesn't grow peas. It only grows coconuts and lemons, so I knew that wasn't true.

Plus you're not allowed to put

children in freezer cabinets. In any country in the world.

I didn't go near the frozen food bit though, just in case. I had to go all the way round the soap powders and along the cereals to find the kitten food. After we'd paid, my mum asked me if I'd like to go to the beach.

But the **trouble with beaches** is they don't have any kittens on them.

So I said no.

Then she asked me if I'd like to walk down to the harbour to look at the boats.

But the **trouble with boats and harbours** is they don't have any kittens in them either.

So I said no.

Then she asked me if I wanted to go and watch the carnival.

But the trouble with carnivals is they don't have kittens in them either.

So we went back to the hotel instead.

After Mum had put the tins of kitten food in our room, she asked me if I wanted to play ping-pong.

But you know the trouble with

ping-pong tables, don't you?

So Mum gave up after that, and told me she was going to the pool bar to talk to Derek.

Which was BRILLIANT! That meant I could go and feed the kittens with Harrison and Jo-Jo.

I couldn't wait to give the kittens their first taste of actual proper Spanish kitten food out of a tin!

Angelo helped me open the tin and then tip it out onto a saucer for them. And he let me chop it up into little pieces with a fork. When the kittens tried it for the first time, you should have heard the purrs

they made. Marble even GROWLED, it tasted so nice!

Angelo told me I was very kind to buy the little *gatitos* proper *gatito* food.

Then the mummy cat told me in cat-speak that I was the kindest person they had ever met. Even kinder than Angelo! Which made me feel really proud!

Then guess what?

Mini Moo asked me if it would be all right if she called me Mum too!

Then all the kittens said it! They all wanted me to be their second mum!

How brilliant was that?!

The mummy cat said she didn't mind one bit if her kittens called me Mum, because I was so kind and because looking after five babies was really hard work. So any help I could give her would be brilliant.

So I decided to help her even more. Because she asked me to.

Because all the kittens asked me to. All five of them.

Plus the mummy cat, which makes six.

WHICH WASN'T MY FAULT!

Chapter 18

I'm not exactly sure which of my mum's screams was the loudest when she woke up in our hotel bed on Thursday morning.

The scream she did when she opened her eyes and found five kittens on the pillows between us . . .

Or the scream she did when she looked in the bathroom mirror.

Both of them were pretty loud.

Very loud actually.

The **trouble with sleeping with kittens** is (and there is NO WAY I could ever have known this) – kittens have fleas.

Especially kittens who live next to dustbins.

The **trouble with fleas** is . . . er . . . they bite.

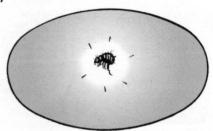

They bite your arms, they bite your tummy, they bite your face while you're asleep, and they make you itchy in all the places they've bitten you.

Except . . .

. . . the **REALLY BIG TROUBLE with flea bites** is (and there is NO WAY I could EVER, EVER have been meant to know this – I mean, EVEN my mum didn't know this until the hotel doctor came and told her . . .) – the **BIGGEST trouble with flea bites** is . . .

. . . my mum's allergic to them!

I'm not. My flea bites were only small and felt a bit itchy. But my mum is absolutely allergic to flea bites **BIG TIME!**

That's why her face had gone all puffy. And the rest of her body too.

"WHAT HAVE YOU DONE TO ME, DAISY?!" she shouted. "I LOOK LIKE THE ELEPHANT MAN!"

Which wasn't true because she didn't have a trunk or anything.

"WHAT ON EARTH POSSESSED YOU TO PUT FIVE KITTENS IN OUR BED?!"

"I was baby-sitting them," I said. "Their mum wanted a night off,

so I said I would help her out. I had
to put them in our bed or they might
have got cold."

But my mum didn't believe me.

"COLD!?" she said. "IT'S THIRTY
DEGREES OUTSIDE AT NIGHT!! HOW
ON EARTH ARE FIVE FURRY KITTENS
GOING TO GET COLD IN THIRTY
DEGREES OF BAKING-HOT SPANISH
NIGHT?!"

So I had to think of another
answer.

"I thought they might get lonely,"
I said.

"LONELY??" she said. "THEY'VE GOT
TEN MILLION FLEAS TO KEEP THEM

COMPANY!! THE ONLY COMPANY
THOSE KITTENS NEED IS A FLEA COMB,
MY GIRL!!!"

Trouble is, then she went back
into the bathroom and looked in the
mirror again.

"LOOK AT MY FACE NOW!" she
said. "IT'S EVEN MORE SWOLLEN!!

"LOOK AT MY EYES!!" she said. "THEY'RE STREAMING! LOOK AT MY CHEEKS!! JUST LOOK AT ME, DAISY!! I'VE GOT A FACE LIKE A BOUNCY CASTLE!!!" she said. Well, shouted, actually.

Trouble is, then she looked at her ankles.

"AND LOOK AT MY ANKLES!" she screamed. "THEY'RE WIDER THAN THE TOPS OF MY LEGS! THIS ISN'T A FLEA ALLERGY – IT'S BUBONIC PLAGUE!"

Which wasn't true either. Otherwise her face would have fallen off. Then she went all thoughtful.

"WAIT A MOMENT," she said. "HOW DID YOU GET FIVE KITTENS IN OUR BED IN THE FIRST PLACE? HOW DID YOU EVEN GET THEM INTO THE ROOM?"

So I told her.

"Harrison helped me lift them up through the window," I said.

"THROUGH THE WINDOW?" she puffed. "HARRISON IS FOUR FOOT TALL, DAISY! OUR WINDOW IS TWENTY FEET ABOVE GROUND LEVEL!"

So then I had to tell her a bit more.

"We put the kittens in my rucksack and then I pulled the rucksack up to our window on a bit of string," I said.

"A BIT OF STRING?" huffed my mum. "WHAT BIT OF STRING?" she puffed.

"I found it by the dustbins," I said.

"RUCKSACKS! WINDOWS! KITTENS! BITS OF STRING!" she said. "AND WHERE WAS I WHEN ALL THESE MILITARY MANOEUVRES WERE GOING ON?"

"You were by the front door, talking to Derek," I said.

"OH MY GOD!" she said, going super puffy now. "I CAN'T GO TO DINNER WITH DEREK LOOKING LIKE THIS!

I CAN'T EVEN LEAVE THE HOTEL ROOM LOOKING LIKE THIS! WHAT HAVE YOU DONE TO ME, DAISY?!"

"It's not my fault the kittens have got fleas!" I said.

"NO, BUT IT'S YOUR FAULT THE

KITTENS ENDED UP IN OUR BED!!"
she said. "ARE YOU MAD,
DAISY? HAS THE SPANISH
SUN SHRIVELLED UP YOUR
BRAINS?!"

The **trouble with talking to mums with huffy puffy faces** is they don't really listen. They just get crosser and crosser.

Especially if then you ask them if you can take five kittens home with you.

Very especially if you do that.

"NO, DAISY, YOU ARE NOT TAKING FIVE KITTENS HOME WITH YOU!" she said. "IN FACT, I'LL TELL YOU WHERE YOU CAN TAKE THOSE KITTENS . . . YOU CAN TAKE THEM RIGHT BACK TO THE FILTHY DUSTBINS WHERE YOU FOUND THEM! IN FACT, YOU CAN PUT THEM IN THE DUSTBIN FOR ALL I CARE!"

So I did.

Not *in. Beside.*

I took them all the way back to the dustbins and put them back next to their number one mum.

I guess that's where they belonged.

Chapter 19

When I told Angelo that my mum had fleas and her face had gone all puffy, he said it might be a good idea if I stayed out of her way for a little while. He said maybe it would be better if I stayed in the pool until her face went down a bit.

But the **trouble with face puff** is it doesn't go down for ages.

Especially when it's flea face puff.

So I decided I'd better go and tell Derek.

"YOU TOLD DEREK WHAT?!" my mum huffed and puffed at me when I finally went back to our room.

"I told him you had fleas," I said.

"YOU TOLD DEREK **I HAD FLEAS**!!!!" she said. "OH MY

WORD . . . THIS JUST GOES FROM BAD TO WORSE!"

"Well, you have, haven't you?" I said. "The doctor said you have."

"THE DOCTOR SAID I HAVE A FLEA ALLERGY, DAISY! HE DIDN'T SAY I HAD FLEAS!!" she said.

"I thought he did," I said.

"OH MY GOD . . . AND HOW MANY OTHER PEOPLE HAVE YOU TOLD THAT I HAVE FLEAS?" asked my mum.

"Only Angelo," I said.

"And Danny and Harrison and Jo-Jo and Carly and Montague and Cerise.

"And Cerise's mum."

The **trouble with telling your mum you've told everyone she has fleas** is even her ears will start to go puffy after that.

And her eyes will go all bulgy.

"BRILLIANT!" she said. (But I don't think she meant it.)

"BRILLIANT BRILLIANT BRILLIANT!! I KNOW, DAISY . . . WHY DON'T WE PUT UP A BIG NOTICE IN THE HOTEL LOBBY AND TELL THE WHOLE WORLD

THAT YOUR MUM HAS FLEAS?"

(But I don't think she meant that either.)

"BEDTIME FOR YOU, MY GIRL AND ROOM SERVICE FOR ME . . . AND TONIGHT, DAISY, YOU CAN SLEEP ON THE SOFA!"

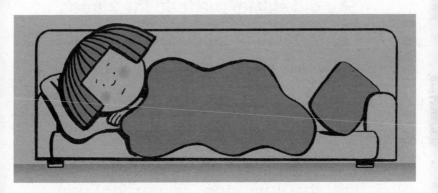

Trouble was, she definitely DID mean that.

Mum didn't come out of our hotel room again after that. Apart from when we had to take our suitcases to the coach on Saturday.

She kept the curtains drawn in our room all day Friday, while I played in the pool with my friends.

She did still let me feed the kittens, but only because she said there was no way we were carrying six tins of cat food home on the plane. And there was no way we were taking five kittens home with us on the plane!

On the last day of our holiday, when I went to say goodbye to the kittens, I thought I was going to cry.

But I didn't.

Angelo made me feel better. He said that Spanish *gatitos* get very shivery in English weather and that the best place for them was here in the warm Spanish sunshine beside the dustbins next to their other mum.

Then he promised me that he would help look after them as well as I had, until I came back to the hotel with my mum, perhaps next year.

When we went home, my mum's ankles were so fat, she had to be pushed in a wheelchair all the way through the airport and lifted up the stairs of the plane.

She wasn't very happy. She said she had wanted to come back from Spain looking like a bronzed beauty but had ended up looking like an over-boiled dumpling.

I told her I was really sorry about the fleas, and if we came back next

year, I would triple promise not to let the kittens sleep with us in the same bed.

But I think her ears were so puffed up she couldn't hear.

Never mind. At least I had a brilliant time!

I found the cutest little *gatitos* in the world!

I learned how to do Spanish cat-speak.

I learned how to play Zombie Mermaids and Zombie Frisbees!

I swapped addresses with Harrison and Jo-Jo before I left so now I can write letters to them whenever I want.

I even learned how to open real kitten-food tins with a tin opener!

But do you know what makes me smile about my holiday more

than anything?

Those clever little *gatitos*, getting me out of going to dinner with that horrible Derek!

Wink, wink!

DAISY'S
TROUBLE
INDEX

The trouble with . . .

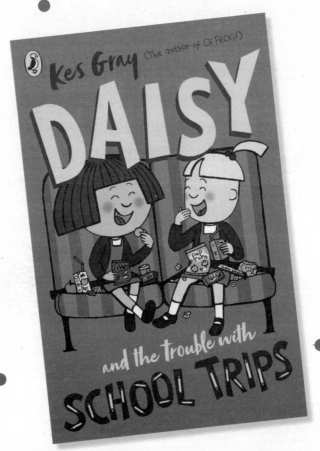